To Lola, Justine, Charlotte, Steph and Clean Cat

American edition published in 2011 by Andersen Press USA, an imprint of Andersen Press Ltd.
www.andersenpressusa.com

First published in Great Britain in 2010 by Andersen Press Ltd.,
20 Vauxhall Bridge Road, London SW1V 2SA.
Published in Australia by Random House Australia Pty.,
Level 3, 100 Pacific Highway, North Sydney, NSW 2060.

Distributed in the United States and Canada by
Lerner Publishing Group, Inc.
241 First Avenue North
Minneapolis, MN 55401 U.S.A.
www.lernerbooks.com

Library of Congress Cataloging-in-Publication Data Available.

ISBN: 978-0-7613-7412-1

Printed and bound in Singapore by Tien Wah Press.
Tony Ross has used watercolor in this book.
This book has been printed on acid-free paper.

1 – TWP – 9/8/10

A Little Princess Story

I Want to Do It Myself!

Tony Ross

Andersen Press USA

"Where are you going, Little Princess?" asked the King.
"I'm going camping," said the Little Princess.

"Let me carry your bags, then," said the Queen.
"No!" said the Little Princess. "I want to do it myself!"

"You can go on my horse!" suggested the General.
"No!" said the Little Princess. "I want to do it myself!"

"My boats will help to take your bags," said the Admiral.
"No!" said the Little Princess. "I want to do it myself!"

And so the Little Princess set off, all by herself
. . . and soon found a beautiful place to camp.

But when she looked in her bags, she found that she had forgotten to bring her tent.

So when the Little Princess went off to find something to use as a tent, the Prime Minister secretly set up his for her.

"Oh bother!" said the Little Princess when she returned.
"I must have brought a tent after all. I am SO forgetful.
I think I will make supper."

But when she looked in her bags, she found that she had forgotten a can opener. She had forgotten a can as well, so she went to look for something to eat.

While she was away, the Cook made a wonderful
supper, ready for her return. Although she could
not remember making it, the meal was very tasty.

"Time for bed!" the Little Princess thought. But she had forgotten to bring a blanket and a pillow. While she was away, looking for something to sleep on . . .

. . . the Maid made up a lovely camp bed.
"Oh BODDLE!" said the Little Princess. "I must
have forgotten I had that."

So the Little Princess tumbled into bed and fell into
a happy sleep. She would have cuddled Gilbert,
if she had remembered to bring him.

In the morning, she looked in her bag for her towel and toothbrush, but she had forgotten to bring them.

Then she spotted them, under a bush.
"I must have put them there in my sleep!" she said.

After her wash, she sat down to think of something to do.

As there was NOTHING to do, the Little Princess packed her bags again and set off home.

"Funny," she thought, "these bags seem heavier than they were yesterday. My stuff must have grown."

On the way back, she met the Gardener.
"Shall I help you with those heavy bags?" he said.

"NO, thanks!" said the Little Princess.
"I want to do it myself!"

When she got home, everyone met her at the gate.
"How was your camping trip?" they asked.

"It was WONDERFUL!" said the Little Princess.
"But I am tired now, because . . .

. . . I DID IT ALL MYSELF!"

Other **Little Princess**
Picture Books

I Want My Light On!
I Want Two Birthdays!

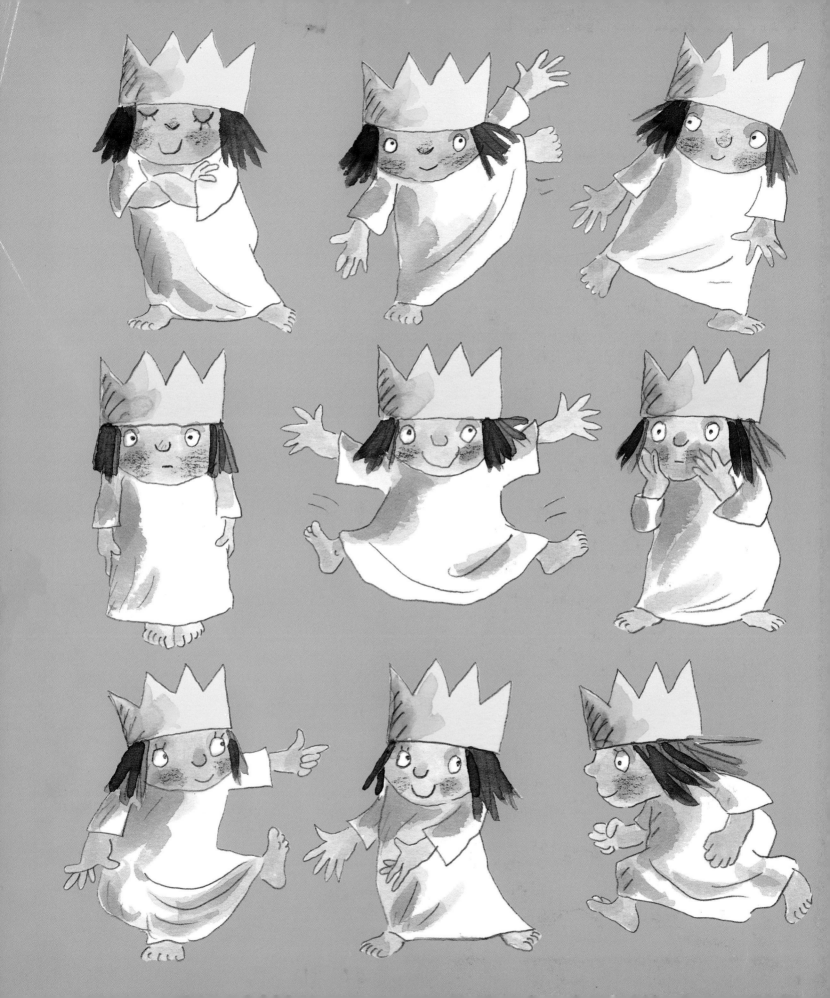